Sins of the Mafia

Contents

Blurb

Four mafia families who rule the underworld. A power struggle that leads to war. And a forbidden love that might set it all ablaze.

Damon

Valachi.

That was the name on my mother's dying lips.

That one word would spark a war.

A war that I planned on winning.

I would go to the Valachi *famiglia*, and integrate myself into their world. I would learn their weaknesses and their secrets, and I would find out who was responsible for my mother's execution.

Then I met Lorenzo Valachi's daughter, Lulu.

She's a queen in the making: strong, beautiful, and full of compassion. She's also an innocent... and the only thing standing in my way.

Lulu lights a fire in me that threatens to burn hotter than my desire for revenge. I can't have her, though—not if I want to avenge my mother.

So, I change my plans, just a little. *I'll have my vengeance, and Lulu, too.*

Lulu

I'm trapped in a golden cage and men hold the key to my freedom.

My father controls his world with an iron fist. When he makes Damon, a made man, his right hand, a light is lit in my darkened world.

He makes me feel things I never thought would be possible.

The closer we get, though, the more I crave. Until one day, he cuts me off and leaves me in the cold.

Only this time I refuse to be silenced. This time I refuse to return to that dark cage.

Damon hasn't just brought light into my world, but hope... ***and hope can be a very dangerous thing.***

CHAPTER ONE

DAMON (SIX YEARS AGO, Palermo, Sicily)

"*F*IGLIO." MY MOTHER TAKES my face in her hands and kisses both of my cheeks. Although an Irishwoman by birth, she always calls me by the Italian word for son in a nod to her Italian husband. It's a bit of respect that pisses me off, as I hold no affection for the man. But in the Mafia world, respect is drilled into us from an early age…beaten into us, in some cases…so I keep my mouth shut and play my part.

"*Madre*. You look younger than ever." I accept her kisses and offer one of my own.

My mother's ruby lips rise into a smile. "Always the charmer, *mio figlio*," she says playfully, and releases my face to take her seat beside my grandmother.

"*Nonna*," I greet my grandmother—my father's mother—who smiles up at me. She's a kind woman, always bearing a smile and a soft word. There was nothing of her in my father, a volatile, angry man. He's gone now, though, so it doesn't matter anymore.

"Damon, you are getting even taller! How is that possible?" Her Italian accent is heavy around the English words.

I walk to her and place a kiss on both of her cheeks. "You say that every time you see me." At twenty-five, I haven't stretched much. My growing days are mostly over with, but my nonna always sees the little changes in me.

"It's the beard," my mother says as I sit down. The blue of her shirtdress matches perfectly with the midday sky.

The view from the restaurant's veranda is picture perfect. With rolling mountains and winding roads that are carved deep, the red caps of the hills make the gray pavements resemble the veins of mountain gods.

The warm Sicily breeze brushes my skin, and I relax in my chair, more at ease than I've been in a while. Maybe it's because my brother, Marcus, isn't joining us today. A mean drunk, he walks in my father's footsteps, so I'm glad I don't have to look at him.

My zia, looks like my mother, with her dark blue eyes and striking black hair. That's where I get my features from—my mother's side. My height and build come from my *padre*. A knot tightens in my chest, and I'm tempted to rub the spot but place my focus somewhere else.

I push a small white box, wrapped tightly with a blue ribbon, toward my Nonna. "A tiny gift," I say.

Her old fingers, coated in rings that weigh her down, reach for the delicate box. Concentration pinches her gray brows as she peels open the ribbon.

"More jewelry?" My *zia* asks before my grandmother has even opened her gift.

"Let her open it, *sorella*. Patience is not a virtue you possess." Madre raises both eyebrows at me and waggles them with good humor.

I hide a smirk. The two sisters are so different—my mother is sweet and gentle, and her sister possesses a wicked tongue and sharp wit. It makes them unforgettable as a duo, and I adore them both. They are women who married hard men, women who gave up their power when they became wives of *la famiglia*.

That's something I learned quickly, when my mother would nurse our wounds or do the best she could by bringing us here for *gelato* after something had happened. But the regret in her eyes was always there, and sometimes, even to this day, I see it peeking out from beneath her lashes.

Nonna struggles with taking the lid off the box, dragging my attention from my thoughts. The anticipation has everyone watching her. I'm hungry, so I reach across the set table and open the lid, revealing the butterfly brooch with a blue stone in the center. The same blue as the ribbon I handpicked only this morning.

Her fingers shake as she brings them to her mouth. "Damon." She hisses my name as she lifts the brooch and brings it closer to her gaze for inspection.

"I had it restored, Nonna."

Her dark blue eyes light as she stares at the gift.

A few years ago, her home, an aging brownstone in the city, had burned to the ground. In it was a brooch passed down from her mother's mother, a family heirloom I knew had to be restored. Finding a man with the talent to bring the jewelry back to life had been a feat in itself, but I had managed to find someone—a man who was close to retirement and happy to take on the task of restoring the object.

"Figlio." My mother is close to tears and reaches across the table to clutch my arm. "I thought it was lost in the fire."

I remember after the fire, when her pain at that loss and others was nearly as great as Nonna's. My grandmother was always more mother to my *madre* than her own kin; my mother was like her own blood daughter. They shared everything as mother and daughter—pain and suffering, joy and pride.

I nod, the gratitude in my mother's gaze almost as rewarding as the awe in Nonna's watery eyes. "It took some time, but it was worth the wait. I'm glad it arrived just in time for Nonna's birthday."

My nonna rises on shaky legs and makes her way around to me. I get up, meeting her halfway. Walking takes a lot out of her, and to have her outside enjoying a meal with us isn't something we thought would even be possible at this stage in her life.

She opens her arms, the brooch held tightly in her clasp. "*Nipote*. My favorite *nipote*."

I laugh and accept her embrace, squeezing her carefully in return. "Don't let Marcus hear you say that."

"I do not care. The world can hear it. He is also my favorite." Nonna looks down at the brooch for a final time, and I don't think she wants me to see the lie in her gaze. She knows what Marcus is; we all know. A carbon copy of our father.

"*Grazie*, Damon." She pats my cheek, and I capture her wrist and place a kiss on the back of her hand.

"You are welcome." I lead her back to her seat.

"Can we eat now? I'm half starved," my *zia* grumbles, and my mother reminds her sister to have manners.

My sister, Evie, and a few of our cousins trickle in just in time for our meal to begin making its way from the kitchen to the table in front of us.

A traditional meal of arancini and seafood risotto is served. I've been away for a time, stuck tending to business matters in Ireland, and I'd all but forgotten how good the food here is. The fragrant odors remind me, and my mouth waters as I wait for Mother to say grace over the meal. At last, we all start to eat. Silverware clinks against china, music plays softly in the background, and cars move along the road below us. All the sounds and smells bring back a million memories of my childhood.

There's always a niggling awareness, though, that hugs the fringes of my consciousness. I find myself glancing around, searching for any potential threat.

There's nothing, of course, but I still have to forcibly remind myself to relax.

Nonna places the brooch back in the white box, and I watch as she winds the blue ribbon around her fingers before placing the box safely in her cardigan pocket. It's too warm for a cardigan, but her illness thins the blood in her body, making her cold even on the hottest days.

"How is Marcus?" my youngest cousin, Sofia, asks. Her hair is pulled up in pigtails—a bit youthful for her fifteen years. She's so like her mother, making us, without a doubt, related. She isn't as sharp-tongued, but she doesn't hide her feelings, either. For example, her dislike for my brother.

I often wonder what he ever did to her. I can only hope it was like nothing he inflicted on me. For a while there, when we were young, we were each other's champions. Allies against the brutality of our world.

He changed, though, at some point. My stomach curls with bitter acid, and I force my demons down.

I force a grin. "He's doing great, I'm sure."

Evie joins in. "It's funny. I was just speaking to him, and he asked about you," she teases our cousin. "Wanted to know if you'd outgrown those pigtails yet."

Sofia rolls her eyes and reaches for her glass of wine, which is acceptable to drink at her age here. In Ireland, that would not be allowed. In Italy, though, we're given wine once we turn ten, so we rarely drink to abuse it. It's simply an extension of the meal for us.

"I'm sure he was," she mumbles into her glass.

My mother's soft laughter is like music to my ears, music I missed badly while spending so much time away from her. She never laughed like that in our youth. Her laughter grew and blossomed once *Padre* was killed, and it was like a bell ringing to signal the end of a war. My body reacts on its own accord, and my shoulders slump slightly.

We make eye contact across the busy table as the chatter continues around us, but it fades as my mother mouths, "*Grazie.*"

I know she means the brooch. Nonna's jewelry will pass to us, the children of her eldest son, when our grandmother dies. Evie always adored the brooch, in particular—she used to play with it when she was a little girl—so I'll make certain it's given to her for her wedding. It's a family heirloom that I'm determined to keep intact.

The noise of the traffic grows louder as my mother turns to my aunt, who's saying something I can't hear. A car sputters below the level of the restaurant, and that little niggle of awareness heightens…turns to tension. I frown while rising, trying to put my finger on what's causing this sudden churning in my gut.

The feeling is inexplicable.

Formless and instinctual.

Without context or meaning, the sound of an exhaust backfiring causes a visceral reaction of my senses and has me moving to investigate.

A flowerpot hanging over our heads shatters, raining a million terra-cotta splinters across the table, and my instinct gains form. It's not an exhaust backfiring but gunshots.

Fucking gunshots.

I dive as screams rend the air, and I retrieve my gun from where I keep it tucked in my waistband.

I'm scrambling along the legs of the table, trying to keep my head beneath its surface. Sofia falls to the beige tiled floor alongside me, covering her head with her hands. Her eyes are tightly closed; her knees drawn up into her belly as another volley of ammunition is fired.

The sound of gunfire sputters to a stop.

I get up, my gaze sweeping the chewed-up table, where food and drink litter the white expanse of the tablecloth. My heart races as red wine turns to blood, and without thought for my safety, I'm up and running, rushing around the table.

Have to check... Have to see...

Faces flash in my mind's eye. Madre. Evie. Nonna...even my aunt and cousins. All of the most precious people in my world.

The waiter bleeds out at my feet. A screech of tires has me stopping at the stone railing, and I fire several shots into the back window of the silver sedan while it peels away, plowing into a couple of pedestrians as it goes. The driver doesn't stop as screams of horror tear through the hot air.

I spin around and drop to my knees. Everyone is on the ground. Nonna is the first person I reach. She's trembling and mumbling incoherent words but seems unharmed, otherwise. My aunt bends over Sofia, trying to calm her down.

Hysterical cries erupt behind me, where Evie curls over the prone figure of my mother. Blood makes a pathway down my sister's face, and I clutch her shoulders, fear gripping me so tightly that the air constricts.

"You're shot—" The words push past numb lips. With a tremble, Evie reaches up and touches her face. She stares at her blood-soaked fingers, shock widening her blue eyes.

"I'm okay...I think it's just..." Her voice trails away as her focus shifts, and she keens, a low, animal sound. Both of us look down at our mother.

Shivers break out across my flesh as I reach across Evie and take in my mother's open hand, her pale fingers dipped in wine.

No, not wine.

Blood.

Lifeless.

I drop the gun and push Evie aside to pull her into my lap. There's so much fucking blood.

"No, no, no..." I freeze as I stare down at the large wound that's torn through flesh and bone. Blood oozes out of it. The cotton fabric of my mother's blue shirt soaks up an alarming amount of blood. Splatters of the sticky red substance coat her neck and face, and dread snaps me out of my frozen state as I look into my mother's dying eyes.

"No, no," I repeat as if I can take this away. Like my words can wield some power that doesn't exist in this realm.

"Madre," I plead.

She swallows. Her blue lips rattle as her limp hand tries to rise.

Her mouth opens and closes, and I lean closer to her. "Save your strength."

My frantic gaze skates around me, taking in the stunned crowd that has gathered to view all the carnage that surrounds us. "Call an ambulance!" I scream at the top of my lungs.

Evie scrambles off the ground, her footsteps unsure as she rises to her feet. Her gaze darts across the destruction on the table. I can only assume she's looking for a discarded phone.

My attention returns to my mother.

My light. She's always been my light.

"Don't speak. Just stay with me. Help is coming." I force a smile before looking up. "Where the fuck is the ambulance?"

The restaurant staff runs around like headless chickens. One male server places the phone back onto the receiver along the tiled wall. "They are on their way."

I turn to my mother. "They're coming. You just have to hold on."

"Damon." My name burbles from her paling lips. Blood oozes, a sluggish river, from the corner of her mouth, and I shake my head.

"Stop speaking." My voice breaks into rusty nothingness, scraped as thin as my soul.

"Valachi." Her final word ends in a gurgle as blood pours from her mouth, and her dead eyes stare up into the cloudless blue of the Sicilian sky.

I shake her. "Madre. Madre—"

Cries unleash around me as the knowledge that my mother has passed reaches my aunt and grandmother.

Pain leeches onto my flesh and sucks the light right out of me, leaving nothing but darkness, agony, and a hunger for revenge.

Valachi.

She must have known they were responsible—why else say their name?

The glint of light on an object catches my attention, and I hold my mother's left hand up. Blood coats the delicate platinum and diamond bridal set, except for a single clear spot that the sunlight blinks obscenely off of. I pull the ring from her finger and close my fist around it. It will belong to my wife one day, a memorial to this woman who raised and nurtured me.

I pull my mother's dead body into my chest, and for the first time since I was six, I cry. I cry bitter, angry tears, and I swear to the gods that I will have my revenge on every Valachi.

They took my mother from me and took my light away.

They will pay.

Dread pools and swirls through my system as I think of the fate I am left with. Our mother declared her oldest son unfit after the death of our father, but this will give him the means he needs to seize power for himself. Power over both the O'Hanlon and Papparado *famiglias*, power over me.

He'll look to restore his birthright, regardless of the damage it could do, and the only person who ever protected us from it is dead in my arms.

Doom drums in the air like a warning of an incoming war.

I believe it.

CHAPTER TWO

LULU (FIVE YEARS AGO, New York City)

*F*AMILY CAN BE SO *mind-numbingly annoying.*

The thought is one of many that rises to the crest of my consciousness as I sit in demure silence on the piano bench.

I'm demure on the outside, at least. On the inside, I'm twitchy with nerves and suppressed energy. I don't want to be here, don't want to deal with whatever it is Father is going to dole out today in the name of the Valachi legacy.

I definitely don't want to put up with our mother, who looks to be about two G&Ts past her limit.

I'd much rather be holed up in my room, listening to the latest Ed Sheeran album and spending time with my sister. Vivi and I could do each other's nails and pretend like we had tickets to his concert later that evening. She'd ask to wear the strappy heels I gifted myself on my birthday last month, and I'd let her because, *Dio sa,* the child never gets to have any fun.

But Father has something he wants to discuss, something important he wants all of us present for. Hence an impromptu, *required* family dinner.

"Isn't that right, Lulu?"

Angel's voice cuts into my thoughts, and I swivel on the bench to face my brother. He's pouring his own drink and giving me a look loaded with meaning. Twenty-seven years old and a *man*, as he's fond of reminding us, he would no doubt prefer to be out with his friends rather than stuck here with his family. Especially since that family just barely manages to tolerate one another most of the time. Except for Vivi and me, of course.

Sometimes I feel like she and I are the only ones who truly care about each other in this household.

"Lu?"

"Hmm?"

I'm not sure what the question was. While awaiting Father's arrival at dinner, Angel and Mother busied themselves with their usual snarking back and forth. I zoned out on their byplay, not wanting any part of it.

Angel tips his head to the side and sucks on his teeth.

"I'm sorry," I say, looking from him to Mother. "I wasn't paying attention."

He rolls his eyes. "Of course, you weren't."

Mother, off in her own little world, makes no comment, and Vivi slumps further into the cushions of the sofa they share before crossing her arms over her chest. It strains at the buttons of the youthful blouse she's dressed herself in, and I make a mental note to take her shopping for more age and figure-appropriate clothing.

"I said, and I repeat, that I bet you know the reason our beloved *padre* has gathered us here in our Sunday finery." A sneer lifts the corner of his mouth before he hides it with his liquor. "Being his little pet and all."

Blood heats my cheeks, mainly because his shot is accurate. I am our father's favorite child, although I don't seek to be.

It also doesn't mean much, being his favored one, except that he likes to show me off, preferring me to escort him to gatherings and events instead of Mother. The world of *la famiglia* here in New York is filled with such social events necessary for showing off one's family, wealth, and power. But there are no perks to the position of favorite child, nothing that makes this life more palatable. Despite the wealth and status of the Valachi name and reputation, I think we are all just a bit unhappy.

Adrift.

"I don't have any idea," I finally answer. "He hasn't said anything to me."

Angel scoffs and tosses his drink back in a single jerky motion before setting the glass down with a solid *thunk* against the table. "You'd say that regardless. I'm sure if you gave it some thought, you could come up with something." His tone turns wheedling. "Come on, Lu. What is it? Exciting new business venture? Someone we need to steer clear of?"

I don't know!

I shout the words mentally but press my lips more tightly together instead of replying.

"You know that whatever it is, he should've told me—"

I can't remain silent. Angel just... doesn't get it. He makes no effort—nothing I've seen, at any rate—to be the man Father requires him to be. If he wants to be involved in Valachi business, at some point he has to grow up. Even five years younger than he is, I'm more of an adult. "I don't have anything to do with that, Angel. Maybe if you didn't sleep until noon and tried to be helpful, he would confide in you more than he does."

Mother shifts suddenly on the sofa, agitation in the wave of her thin hand. "Viviana, do sit up straight and stop flopping about on the couch. Your hunched posture is doing nothing to slim you, you know." Her mouth turns down, faintly disgusted.

Vivi casts a wounded glance in my direction, but she dutifully pulls herself taller without argument, settling the tips of her slippered feet onto the textured rug that covers the hardwood. My jaw tightens as I watch. Vivi exploded into budding adulthood almost overnight, just days shy of her sixteenth birthday, an... enthusiastic... bloomer after years where we were beginning to wonder if she'd ever get her first period, ever develop.

She's developing with abandon now, bursting from her childish cocoon into what I imagine will be Sophia Loren-style glory.

Mother seems to be chronically put out by her recent rapid changes, though. Instead of helping her navigate her foray into womanhood, she acts as though it's an embarrassing curse Vivi brought upon herself and the family.

I've been the one to teach my sister about her body, about everything that's happening to her. And for the most part, she's good with her development—until Mother starts spouting stupidities like she is now. While Vivi's breasts came in seemingly overnight and with voluptuous inhibition, she still carries a bit of baby fat, making her appear overweight to someone inclined to be cruel or someone with no imagination.

Not that I want anyone imagining any sort of thing about my little sister.

Her lush frame does nothing to detract from what is plain to any observer—Vivi Valachi will one day be a stunning woman.

In fact, sometimes I think it's jealousy that makes our mother snipe at her, because it's clear—to me, at least—that one day her youngest daughter will be far more beautiful than Nina Valachi, lounging there now in all of her alcohol-soaked misery.

I refuse to give that misery the company it craves. "Mother—"

The double-hung mahogany doors to the drawing room swing open abruptly, cutting off what I was about to say. Sending Vivi a commiserating look, I turn my attention to Father and the young man he ushers in with him before pulling the doors closed once again.

Young-ish, anyway. He's definitely older than my twenty-two years, but younger than many of Father's made men. And handsome. Even though I'm not interested, because it would be a veritable death sentence for him if I were, I can't help but notice that fact. It's all... *right there*. In front of me.

I eye him from beneath my lashes as Father begins to speak.

He's tall. Taller than Angel, even, who stands nearly a foot higher than my own five feet three inches. His hair is dark, his skin an unusual blend of pale with olive undertones. Is he Italian? I can't quite tell. His gaze roves, as curious about us as I am about him. It brushes each person in the room briefly before landing on me. His eyes begin to slide past me, then pause and return, narrowing as he returns my perusal.

I shiver.

His eyes are the blue of a deep, dark ocean when the sunlight cuts through it, electric in their intensity.

I can feel them.

It's like... I struggle for context long after he pulls his gaze from me and turns to my father, finally finding a way of explaining the sensation to myself when he's no longer studying me. It's like when a freezing raindrop manages to find its way beneath the collar of my coat, slithering down my neck and along my spine.

Cold, bright lightning.

I quell a second shudder of sensation and focus on Father.

"...Damon Papparado. He's going to be lending me his assistance from here forward. I know you will all afford him the respect—"

Papparado. Italian, then. The name is familiar to me, the Papparados being a comparatively minor *famiglia*. Most of them are still located in Sicily, but there are a few here in New York. Although small, they're powerful in their own right in Italy, and I'm fairly certain my father has done business with them.

My brow contracts with confusion as I run through what I know, one thing standing out above everything else. He's bringing someone we've never met before into our home, our lives, to... assist? Assist with what?

I can't help the rush of irritation at his seeming callousness. What about me? Have I not been there for every one of his requirements, taking care of every family need when he's not available? Have I not played peacekeeper ad nauseam between Angel and Mother? Mother to his youngest daughter?

Angel doesn't seem to care for Father's announcement, either.

"What the hell is this?" He leaps to his feet from where he had seated himself earlier, all of his careful indolence vanishing from his posture to reveal his agitation more plainly than any words. "You're bringing some stranger into the fold, and you want me to respect him? Without any warning, or... or..."

Father's expression hardens. "You forget yourself, *mio figlio*."

It's all he says, but we're neither deaf nor stupid; we hear the unspoken words. The tension between Father and Angel has clamored in this household for decades, and tonight is no different.

Sit down.

Behave.

Remember your place.

Angel's face reddens, and he draws himself up, stiff with anger. "It is my job to be your right hand, Papa." His voice thins with emotion he swiftly suppresses, except for the fist he thumps against his chest. "My duty." He approaches Damon, glaring a challenge until he's standing toe to toe, and touches his fist lightly to Damon's chest. "*My* honor."

Damon's upper lip curls, but he makes no reply.

"Angel—" I don't know what I intend to say. It doesn't matter because Angel has turned back to face our father and is speaking again.

"I will do as you ask," he says. "But I won't pretend it is not the greatest insult you could have dealt me."

As Father sputters, Angel strides from the room, rage an echo trembling in his wake.

"My apologies, Papparado—" Father begins.

Damon waves a hand. "It is nothing. I expected some growing pains." He slants a look at us, clearly wanting to say more, but he must think better of it, because he smiles slightly instead.

The room, silent for a moment, feels heavy. Father looks at me and lifts an eyebrow, the command silent but obvious.

I rise from the piano bench and clasp my hands lightly before me. "I'll just go see if the meal is ready."

Mother's fingers reach for my arm as I glide past. I pause, looking down at her as she sits beside my sister. "Who's the fancy lady now?" she says, the words slurring slightly. "Why don't you keep to your place and sit down?"

I close and open my eyes in a slow blink. She's gone from buzzed to drunk in minutes, it seems. Father is speaking intently with Damon Papparado, unaware of his wife's state. Papparado sees, though, his eyes resting on us even as he answers a question.

"I guess we're just going to air all our dirty laundry tonight," I mutter and tug gently at my arm as I continue to leave the room.

She's not finished and wrenches me closer. The other hand, the one with the drink in it, flails with the motion, and gin sloshes out to splash Vivi.

"Mother!" she shrieks, lifting her hands to wipe at the alcohol staining her face and chest.

"*Dio santo*. I am surrounded by imbeciles!" Father marches toward the door, done with the lot of us.

I'm not concerned with him. At Vivi's squawk, a feral kind of fury crosses our mother's face, and she rears back, her hand holding the glass raised to strike.

I don't think. I don't hesitate. I just move, allowing the momentum of having her other hand on my arm carry me forward, in between her and Vivi. There's a muffled exclamation—Papparado's, I think— and then a rush of pure, blinding pain as the glass collides with my temple.

And then there's nothing at all.

CHAPTER THREE

DAMON

CRUELTY IS PART OF our world. It comes with the territory of the Mafia, be it Italian, Irish, Russian... any of the syndicates. We expect violence from men. It's a necessary evil, unless you want to look weak, like dying prey, easy pickings for the superior male.

I understand violence.

Fuck me, I've been on the end of such more than I care to admit.

But seeing the oldest girl, Luciana-called-Lulu, tumble to the ground makes something primal rise inside me. I have never felt protective of anything or anyone outside my family... so why are my feet rushing toward her?

My black polished shoes thud loudly on the hard wooden floor, then are silenced as I cross the Persian rug and stop where she's crumpled on the floor. I look down at her, and even though she stirs something protective in me, I'm also aware of how easily I could crush her. How truly helpless she is lying beneath my feet.

The mother tuts, drawing my attention. Her cruelty is something I hadn't expected. Even in our vicious world, women are demure, silent, the men's lesser halves. That is the normal way of things with our women; the ones who rise up and show even a molecule of power get shot down.

Just like Madre.

I blink, the pain still unbearably fresh. A full year hasn't dulled my pain or my desire for revenge. It's why I'm standing here in the Valachi's drawing room.

All roads lead here.

I had decided I would keep an open mind. After all...it was only one word on the lips of a dying woman, and there were things that simply didn't make sense. She could have possibly meant something different than "the Valachis are responsible." She could have meant...*merda*, I don't know. All I know is that while I want my revenge, I also want the *right* revenge. I need to be sure.

But Marcus had informed me of some vague threats he had intercepted, chatter about the growing might of the O'Hanlons and how a woman, my *madre*, was leading them.

She had kept her involvement in things quiet, but it was not inconceivable that it had been discovered. Her presence at the O'Hanlon helm, joining the biggest syndicate in Ireland with a smaller, but no less influential family like the Papparados, would not have been good for the Valachis. An alliance with the wrong person in charge made both families too strong. A Valachi response to this made sense.

But I still needed to know for certain. Because why would Lorenzo Valachi invite me into his home, invite me to become his made man, if he had just had my mother murdered? Was he that arrogant?

This violence, springing from the Valachi *madre* herself, is confirmation. They are animals, these people.

Every night for the past year, I've been ripped from sleep, my mother's dying word ringing in my head. *"Valachi."* They had succeeded in putting my mother into the ground, but they had no idea how her death would ignite my blood like a flint sparking flame to tinder.

I swore I would cut everyone involved down, and yet here I stand over one of their offspring, feeling this curious sense of protectiveness.

Why? I can't spare her. Can't spare any of them, not if they're responsible. I won't.

"Leave her," Nina Valachi tells me, the stink of liquor wafting from her breath. "I barely touched her. As always, Lulu loves being dramatic." Her mother's eyes roll back with the effects of the drink, and her attention moves back to her original target, the youngest Valachi, Vivi.

The mark on the side of Luciana's face is not the result of a slight tap, though. A purpling lump is forming fast, and the girl's gaze is unfocused as she lifts a hand to brush the site where the heavy lowball crystal made contact.

"Are you okay?" My voice sounds strained and angry, which isn't my intention.

My heart says help her, while my brain tells me to leave her on the ground—one less Valachi to take down. The conflicting emotions have me standing stiffly.

Her head rises, her swanlike neck craning back as she blinks rapidly at me. How easily I could stand on her neck and crush bones.

"Look what you did," the mother accuses Vivi. She points at Lulu on the floor, and when Vivi doesn't follow her manicured finger, instead staring at her in horror, she reaches across and grabs the young woman's chin, forcing her to look at her sister.

"Look what you've done," she repeats, as if Vivi was a puppeteer and manipulated her mother's violence toward Lulu.

"I'm okay." The words emerge as a hoarse whisper, Luciana all but swallowing them. "It's okay, Mother."

She reaches out a delicate hand to find her balance as she tries to get to her feet. I'm wiser than my actions right now as I lean down and take her by the elbow, filled with the awareness that I should just leave her.

At the contact, Lulu stills, her uncertain gaze stretching up to meet mine. God, she's so young. Early twenties, maybe, which is not a child, and yet it's likely she's been so fiercely protected her entire life as to render her completely innocent. I need to leave her alone.

A muscle ripples in my jaw, and I'm debating releasing her when she moves, allowing me to help her to her feet.

I want to ask her again if she's okay, but then I remember why I'm here. My fingers slide from her slim arm.

Luciana runs her hands down the front of her dress as if she's brushing out wrinkles that aren't there. She raises her head, and her expression, as she turns to her mother, sends shivers down my spine.

Formidable. I've seen that look before, a very long time ago, and my eyes narrow. Her strength reminds me of my mother.

I suspect Lulu Valachi might well be a worthy opponent... or prize. Perhaps even a possession. A smirk tugs at my lips, but I suppress it.

"I'll just check on Angel." Despite the ruthlessness in the glance she sends her mother, Lulu's footfalls are unsure, like those of a newborn deer.

She leaves and I glance at the mother, whose eyes are at half-mast. The alcohol is doing its job. Vivi sits with her head bent, her hands in her lap. She won't look up, and she won't leave, either. I'm surprised she hasn't followed her sister out of the room to make sure she's okay, but clearly, they're not crafted of the same fibers.

It makes me think of Marcus and our childhood, which had been painted in blood and pain. Our father enjoyed the bottle just like Lulu's mother. Funny how I ended up in a house just like my own. When our *padre* favored his belt as a form of discipline, we took the beatings he delved out regularly without argument, knowing that doing so would only make things worse.

He loved to hear us scream.

It was after the abuse when we were the strongest. If it had been me on the end of our *padre's* violence, Marcus would stay with me, making me laugh through my pain. And vice versa. If it was Marcus's flesh torn from the steel of the belt buckle, I would stay with him. I wasn't much for jokes, but I had the best stash of comic books, and we would read them together. I always leaned toward anti-heroes like Venom. And Rorschach from Watchmen—he was someone I could understand, as his childhood of abuse had led him down his own destructive path.

Carnage, ironically, was Marcus's favorite. He wasn't far into his teenage years before he began exhibiting a similar kind of instability and lust for destruction.

I'm pulled from the memory as Lulu's mother mumbles something incoherent but clearly nasty, and frankly, I've seen enough.

I have no one to give departing words to, as Valachi left the room following his wife's casual display of violence, so I leave, closing the doors behind me and shutting Vivi in with her mother.

The long, empty hallway is silent. My gaze is drawn to the double staircase that dominates its width, but a noise further down the corridor has me stepping in that direction. Overhanging arches appear every twenty feet, the intricate baroque design along the edges making it appear as if the arch is about to drip water down upon me. Paintings wrapped in gold frames flank both sides of the arches; the splendor screams wealth and power and gives me a sense of oppression at the same time.

It's too much. I much prefer my own home, an apartment in Cobble Hill, New York.

Light slits the oak flooring beneath my feet. The source is a partially open door tucked into an alcove. I raise my hand to knock but pause before pushing the door noiselessly open and stepping in.

It's a miniscule bathroom, probably used for servants or unimportant guests, judging from the lack of opulence. Everything else in this house is luxurious and extravagant, so this small room doesn't seem like one the family would be accustomed to using. Yet, it's here where I find Lulu.

Her hands are clasped on either side of a white pedestal sink, her face turned away from me as she examines the lump on her head in a mirror hung above the sink.

"My *nonna* always recommended butter to take down the swelling."

Her head snaps in my direction, and she appears immobilized for a brief second before, like a clumsy deer, she releases the sink and fights to find her balance. Like a spinning top, she tilts, and I take a step toward her. When she rights herself, I stop.

Her nostrils flare, and she tilts her head. Her hand rises to the lump on her temple. "Butter?" Her voice is all soft, feminine grace, and more anger floods my bloodstream. I'm wondering why the fuck I'm sharing such private information with her.

"Yes. I'm not sure what properties are in butter, but whenever I got a bump, she would slather it with butter." I want to smile at the memory of Nonna taking down the cream porcelain butter dish. She would remove the lid, dip two fingers into the yellow substance, and smother the hurt with it. I don't smile, though. Instead, another wave of loss tightens my hands into fists. Nonna died before her ninety-sixth birthday, leaving me without a mother or grandmother.

"Did it work?" she asks.

I'm aware of how close we're standing, of how I tower over her.

"It definitely made me feel better," I confess, stretching out my fingers. If Nonna had ever suspected the beatings our father gave us, she would have been beside herself. She hadn't raised him to be a violent man, but the life... it tends to make us so. No amount of butter could heal the wounds that were inflicted upon our psyches.

Lulu's hazel eyes soften further, gold flecks swirling, and I find myself looking away. She shouldn't look at me like that. If she had a lick of sense, she'd be running.

"I'll try some. Thank you."

I nod. I shouldn't be chasing after the first pretty thing I see, even if I do like to collect things of beauty. Maybe I will add Luciana Valachi to my collection.

I smirk as I take a step, crossing the threshold. "Try the butter." My departing words are rough.

As I leave the dark beauty in the bathroom and track down her piece of shit father, I remind myself why I am here.

To avenge my mother. To inflict a debilitating level of pain on the Valachi family, as they did upon ours.

That was my sworn promise. And having more power than Marcus is a strong driver, as well. I don't trust him. The thought propels me down the hallway.

Time to get to work.

CHAPTER FOUR

LULU

T IME PASSES IN A blur. Damon's arrival has done so much for our family. Father no longer relies on Angel or me to the extent he once did. Damon has taken on our roles, and others, with ease, and yet somehow, he's managed to keep himself separate from all of us.

All of us, that is, except for Vivi. He likes her, treats her as an affectionate older brother would.

For the first time in what feels like forever, a garden is blooming in the Sahara of my soul.

It started slowly—a single, fragile shoot rising through the parched earth of days spent avoiding Mother and bending to Father. With every furtive glance Damon sends my way, every shock of sensation created by the accidental brush of our skin, it gathered momentum, and now it's planted firmly even as it reaches for the light.

Damon.

Damon is the light.

There's no way, though, that anything between us would ever work. He's so much older—older than Angel, even. More significantly, he's my father's man. Any kind of dalliance with the don's daughter would be death to a man in the employ of *la famiglia*—not because Father loves me, particularly, but because he *values* me.

My lips thin and twist, and I pound a fist once, twice into the sticky dough I'm working with. He values what I can bring him.

I've long since moved past the point of being angry about my father. I am Valachi, the eldest daughter. As such, I will eventually be married to someone who brings my family something they need, something that will make them stronger. That's simply the way of things in our world.

I managed to get Father to hold off on any such arrangement, making myself indispensable to him and playing on his need for me. Until Damon, Father relied on me to keep things even keel with the family and serve as a kind of partner, as Mother is less than useless. She's a liability.

I pinch off a tiny piece of dough and bring it to my mouth, closing my eyes and humming a bit at the tart, slightly sour flavor.

God, I love bread.

This is not the existence I fantasized about as a child. I wanted to be a pastry chef and maybe something fun, like an event coordinator. Father didn't allow me to go to culinary school, despite years of pleas.

It was too dangerous, he said.

I would be a target, he said

Someone might steal me to get to him, he said.

No... best I stay home like a good girl and let Father keep me safe. And so here I remain at the ripe old age of twenty-two, performing tasks a wife should be, taking care of a father and family who don't deserve my affection. Although... it's not like I don't have the time, I suppose.

I have nothing but time, stretching out before me, dull minute after dull minute, confined as I am to my golden cage.

Poor little mafia princess, I sneer at myself. I don't think I'll ever be free.

Still, I can't help wishing on the star I cannot reach. Can't help dreaming of having a life I create for myself, of days I walk through with autonomy, doing things I choose for myself.

With a snort, I move to the next loaf. From my spot at the marble counter beneath the wall of steel-framed windows, I watch Damon with my sister. My hands stay busy, kneading and folding the wet mixture that will become several fresh loaves of ciabatta. The automatic nature of the task gives me the excuse I need to focus on the man beyond the glass.

He would catch any woman's eye. It's certainly no hardship to allow myself space to moon a little over his strongly formed, handsome features, using the cover of watching Vivi. He's not conventionally good-looking. His face doesn't possess pretty-boy perfection, but that's what I like about it. It has character, shaped by things like the faintly cruel set of his mouth and the way it's at odds with the emotion I see constantly roiling in those dark blue eyes.

His face—no, scratch that—*the man* fascinates me. It's a dangerous allure, one I know I should ignore with every ounce of will within me.

What really captivates me, more than his looks or the sensual masculine grace he moves with, is the way he interacts with my sister when he thinks no one's looking.

This is why he's the light.

My hands pause their task, resting motionless on the dough, as the housekeeper enters. "Miss?"

"Yes, Gina?"

The round woman wrings her hands before her. "I... I'm not sure I should say anything—"

"Speak freely, please."

Her face is creased with worry. "It's your brother, Miss. He's just come home and is throwing things around in your father's office..."

I sigh. "I'll take care of it. Thank you for letting me know, Gina."

She leaves, and I return to my task, shaking my head a little. It's not the first time Angel's come home and thrown a tantrum over something, and it won't be the last. I'll tend to it in a while. After I finish the bread... and finish watching Damon from the window. I'm always watching him from a distance. He might give Vivi some of his time, but he doesn't share the same space with me. I think he does his best to avoid me, really. It's been this way ever since the night my mother hit me in front of him. Those were the most words we have shared.

Right now, he and Vivi sit on the wicker patio couch, appearing to be engaged in a playful debate that involves a thumb war. Vivi is laughing, her face tipped back and open to the sun. For once, it's empty of the chronic anxiety she battles when our parents are around.

He did that. Damon gave her this beautiful confidence by spending time with her, listening to her teenage agonies, and making her laugh.

It gives me hope.

I don't think too far beyond that. Hope for what? I don't want to name it. Doing so would give this tendril of feeling life and substance beyond this moment, and for my own sanity, I can't allow that.

As if he's in sync with my thoughts, Damon's gaze lifts and snags mine through the window. He tips his chin the slightest bit, acknowledging me silently, and I send a tremulous smile in response. I lift my hand from the dough before me, intent on acting normal and waving, when something shatters on the floor behind me and makes me jump.

Whirling around, I utter a low moan when I spy my next bowl of dry ingredients coating the island and floor, along with two of the loaves I'd just prepped for rising. Angel paces back and forth through the mess, tugging at his dark hair.

"Angel! What on earth—"

He jerks a hand at me, cutting me off. "Don't start with me, Lu. I'm not in the mood."

"I can see that!" I want to wail. He's ruined my bread. No time to be upset about it, though. I have to calm the raging beast.

I slide into the spacious pantry and mudroom area to find the broom, but more significantly, to give myself a moment to take a deep breath and count to ten. "Serenity now," I murmur, channeling one of my favorite syndicated television shows, and then grab the broom and return to the kitchen. "What happened, Angel?"

He drops into a chair at the island bar and stares gloomily at his hands. "What do you think?"

I squint over at him as I sweep ineffectually at the spread of flour on the aged brick floor. I have a pretty good idea of what brought him raging into my sanctuary and knocking things around. His name is Lorenzo, and he goes by Father.

"Let's see..." I muse, striking a playful pose with a finger to my chin. "It's either the dealership was out of the newest Maserati, or Cook forgot to pick up that awful cocoa-flavored cereal you like, or—"

Angel snorts a laugh in spite of the anger that still lingers in the stiff lines of his body. This is my most important job, perhaps—peacekeeper. There's always some ugliness that needs smoothing over, some hurt that needs mending. He sobers almost instantly, scrubbing his hands over his face. "No," he says. "All that's fixable."

I frown. "Everything can be fixed, *fratello*. Talk to me."

"I—" With a shake of his head, Angel clamps his lips closed.

"What the hell happened here?" On a gust of cool wind, the French door to the terrace opens, and Damon sweeps in, followed by Vivi. He eyes the carnage of flour and dough with flinty eyes.

Damn it. I'm sure Damon is only trying to help, but this confrontation is sure to make things worse. My eyes beg him to retreat.

Angel rises, a sneer on his lips. "Nothing for you to worry about, *stronzo*. Run along back to daddy. Oh, wait... that would be *my* daddy, wouldn't it?"

Vivi gasps, turns on her heel, and walks back outside. I don't blame her. She's as non-confrontational as can be and will do anything to avoid a disagreement.

There's a nearly imperceptible hardening of Damon's generally hard-to-read expression. Instinctively, I know whatever happens next will not go well for my brother. I take a half step forward, reaching out a hand. "Okay, let's not do this, please—"

"Get out of the way, Lu." Angel draws himself up to his full height, his bristle-covered chin jutting forward. Damon says nothing, merely watches with a gaze I can only think of as predatory.

Awareness floods me. *He wants this*, I realize. He's itching for it.

"No." I place a hand on Angel's chest and gently push him backward. "You're not doing this, Angelus Christiano." I use his full name to try to jog some response other than this willful desire to brawl, but he ignores me.

"Luciana." I turn around at Damon's interruption. He doesn't look at me, instead keeping his gaze focused on my brother. On the threat.

"Damon—" I start.

"Luciana, it would be best if you left the room, now."

Tears threaten, and I bite my lip, hard, to quell them. "You can't be serious."

He looks at me at that. "I don't joke, *bella ragazza*."

Pretty girl. My cheeks heat with a furious blush. I'm about to reply, to tell him *it's fine, I have everything under control*, when Angel butts in, shouldering me a step back and into Damon. His hands come up reflexively, settling on my upper arms.

"You don't look at *mi sorella*," Angel bites out.

"Oh, *mon Dio*." Pulling free of Damon's grip, I shove my brother. "Out! Out of my kitchen! You come in here, throwing yourself around and having your little fit. Messing up my work. I've had it, Angel. Go!" He stares at me, silent only a moment before his lips part. I hold up my hand, cutting him off. "You can't ever leave well enough alone. Always have to have the last word." My voice cracks—I hate this eternal fighting. It's ceaseless. I'm so weary of it. "I don't want to hear it. I'm done."

I swipe angrily at my eyes. "Go, damn it!"

Angel pivots without another word and strides away. Damon doesn't move. His heat at my back surrounds me when he brings his hands up once again to take my biceps in a firm grip. "That goes for you, too." I sniff. "You're just as bad, encouraging that macho nonsense."

"You don't mean that," he says, tugging my back against his chest in an embrace that contradicts itself. I can feel the struggle in the tension of his grip, like he wants to hold me and push me away at the same time.

I can help him make that decision.

I pull away, trying desperately not to let loose the tears that crave freedom. I need to be alone. "I do mean it," I say, turning around to face him. "This...you just made everything worse. I had it handled."

He doesn't reply immediately, simply traces his bottom lip with his forefinger and watches me with brooding eyes. Then he speaks. "If I tell you to do something, *bella*, I expect you to listen. I'm doing it for your own good. This wasn't about you. You didn't need to have it handled, not with me here to do that for you."

I sputter. "You're not the boss of me, Damon! You're not my father! It's not your place to do these things—" I break off, holding up a hand when his lips part on an argument. I don't want to listen. I won't. "I want you to go, Damon. I want you to leave me alone and for God's sake—stay out of private family business in the future!"

With a finger that shakes only a little, I point at the door.

Damon's eyelids hood his gaze, but not before I see something spark in the depths of his eyes. "I don't think you mean that at all, *bella*."

Merda.

Too late, I realize I've messed up. I stood my ground, had my say, and in doing so, I waved a red flag in a Pamplona bull's line of sight.

I close my eyes briefly, finally allowing a single tear to track its way down my cheek.

This isn't a fight I'm going to win.

CHAPTER FIVE

DAMON

I've never seen Luciana fall apart.

Every petty act of violence by her mother, every careless word from her brother or father...they don't faze her. She raises her head, and her gaze fills with a restrained defiance I had only ever seen before in my *madre*. I admired that discipline, found myself wanting to nurture it, wanting to give Lulu the nourishment and strength she needs to become the Queen she is meant to be.

And yet, seeing this Queen finally break and cry makes me feel like a King.

I've caused that depth of pain inside her, and that knowledge fills me with a twisted thrill. Knowing I caused the tears shouldn't elate me, but each tiny, pain-filled drop does exactly that. It thrills me that I've brought her to this point, so far from her norm.

She's right that I should leave. I normally walk away from anything that could entwine me with Lulu, but today, I want to play with her a little. In my head, she is mine; she just doesn't know it yet. But I've decided that no one will ever possess this woman—only me, and only when the time is right.

"I don't think you want me to leave, *bella*." I take a step toward her. Lulu's cheeks are flushed, flour is sprinkled down the front of her dress, and a white mark on the side of her head has me reaching up and dusting the flour away. "You have flour in your hair," I inform her.

She holds her breath at my closeness. Her head tilts to the side, her long neck begging for the brackets of my hands. My gaze moves upward, past that flawless flesh, and my gaze dips to her pouty lips. She's normally careful, but today those lips fired off her every thought. How freeing it must be to speak your mind, consequences be damned. I'll have to work on that. Lulu's fiery nature is alluring but also concerning at times.

My hand leaves her hair, and my fingers trace a path through her tears. Her eyelids flutter closed, and she inhales a breath. "Damon." The word is a plea.

I bring my fingers to my lips and taste salt. I taste her pain, and it's so fucking sweet.

My cock is hard, unyielding against my trousers. The thought of having Lulu tortures me every night. I can picture fucking her across the flour-stained counter. Burying myself inside her sweet pussy... one I know that no man has yet to touch and never will.

She would be tight. I nearly groan at the thought of being her first, her only, and torment clenches my teeth against a groan.

Merda. She's everything I never expected to want, everything I can't have, every-fucking-thing that stands in the way of my purpose... and yet, I can't stop feeling the way I do.

A strand of her hair moves as my breath fans out across her face. Fuck, I want her so bad. Since arriving here and seeing her courage, I've obsessed over Lulu Valachi without pause.

I have to taste her.

It's a split-second decision that causes me to press my lips against hers. Lulu's eyes remain open, her mouth frozen under mine, and there's a second where dread floods my veins and I think I've read every signal wrong.

But when her hands rest on my chest, and she parts her mouth, a tentative acceptance, I don't pause but force my lips hard against hers.

My hand glides to her waist, and I propel her backward until the small of her back is pressed against the countertop. She tastes so fucking perfect. Her tongue flicks out into my mouth, and my cock becomes even heavier and more painful in my boxers. Gripping her face in my hands, I tilt her head, allowing me full access to her mouth. My tongue slides in and dances with hers.

When I push my body against hers, she freezes, her breath harsh. I nudge her with my hips, letting her feel my erection against her stomach and watching the expressions dance across her face.

Fear.

Lust.

Excitement.

They send a thrill throughout my body.

A movement in the hall has me stepping back and searching the hallway beyond the entrance to the kitchen. I see no one, but that means nothing.

Still cupped in my hands, Lulu's face creases in bewilderment, and I realize that while I was kissing this girl, my lust for her burned brighter than my need for revenge ever did.

Unacceptable.

Fear of forgetting why I'm here has me stepping away from her. I will have her, just not right now. Her finely-boned hand flits up to her mouth, red and swollen from my kisses.

I clench my jaw. This can't happen. If I let it continue, Lulu will ring the death knell on my vow of vengeance. Her eyes burn into mine, asking a question I have no answer for.

Never again. I'm already obsessed with Lulu but tasting her has sent my body into a spiral. A spiral I fear I will fall into and never return from.

"My *madre* would have loved you." I speak the painful truth as I depart the kitchen. I won't touch Lulu Valachi again. Not until I have what I came for.

Running my hands through my thick hair as I go, I notice I have flour on my shirt from where Lulu pressed herself against me. I brush the white powder off and pause as a set of legs appears in my periphery. My gaze travels the length of legs to the face of their owner, another Achilles' heel.

"Won't you come and sit with me?" Vivi asks, using her sweetest, most wheedling voice. Five minutes ago, I was outside with her. Laughing. I had, after all, won five thumb wars in a row. She wasn't happy about it, and I'm sure she wants a rematch.

I look at her, feeling helpless. Like Lulu, Vivi has found a way to slowly thread herself through my broken heart. The sisters could have the power to heal me, but that comes hand in hand with the power to destroy. I faced that kind of destruction once; I won't do so again.

"I have work to do," I say to Vivi without meeting her gaze. I set my jaw, keeping myself from saying anything else.

She sighs dramatically. "Is this because I let you win?"

I glare at her, ready to tell her I won fair and square, when a slow smile spreads across her face. She was hoping for this reaction. Vivi's confidence has come a long way in the last few months that I have been here. I don't want to hurt her. I don't want to undo even one fiber of confidence that has been woven into the girl. She's an innocent, despite being a Valachi, and so very young. I'll do everything I can to leave her whole.

But I can't allow her access to me anymore. "I don't want to play, Vivi. I have work to do."

I walk past her, but not before I see the hurt latching onto her shoulders and dragging them down. Tightening my hands into fists, I refuse to stop or pivot or tell her I take my words back. I want to run out and declare a rematch just to see her face light up with glee. I want to erase the sorrow I just caused, and I could do so—in a heartbeat.

I have that kind of power.

It's a power I would no longer use, though, because in the long run, it would be a disservice. Sometimes you have to be cruel to be kind.

My room is in the north tower of the house. The towers are not very tall, only three stories in height, but they serve their purpose in keeping me separate from the rest of the house and its occupants. While he likes the things I do for him, Lorenzo has always been firm that I am on the payroll and not part of his family. At first, I loved the seclusion, but as time passed and I grew closer to the girls, I found myself seeking them out. That will have to stop.

I cross through the arched doorway and walk to the elongated window overlooking the back lawns. There, beneath the oak tree, is Vivi, tapping away at her cell phone. I spin away from her and lick my lips, tasting Luciana and bitterness.

I had wanted to fuck her so badly. If she had encouraged me the slightest bit further, I wouldn't have been able to stop. Closing my eyes, I inhale deeply, scenting the sweet floral fragrance that still clings to my clothes. I can almost picture her standing in front of me with flour in her hair and tears on her cheeks.

My cock is swollen, and my erection begs to be touched. I walk to the bathroom and strip off my clothes. Turning on the water and stepping into the shower, I allow the spray to stream across my body and give in to the carnal need that has taken over me.

Eyes closed, I hiss as I stroke my cock. If I try, I can picture Lulu's small hands wrapped around my cock, her mouth struggling to take all of me, but I would try to push my cock down her throat anyway, fucking her sweet face.

My balls tighten as I pump my cock into my hand, imagining it's Lulu's mouth. How fucking beautiful would she look kneeling at my feet, her hand and mouth working my cock? A princess on her knees. Her lips would tighten around my shaft as I pounded into her mouth, the soft, wet flesh stretching to take me. Her large breasts would be free, and I could picture her hard nipples reacting eagerly to each brush against my legs, sending waves of pleasure throughout her and making her work harder on my cock, her warm, wet mouth sucking vigorously.

I'm pulling my cock harder. It throbs with each stroke, pre-cum coating the top of my fingers, and I use it as a lubricant to rub around the swollen head. My balls hang, full to the top with cum that I want to spray across Lulu's face and tits. That's the image that has me jerking harder and faster. She would open her mouth and welcome my cum. Her tongue would be waiting eagerly to taste me. My hand slams against the shower tiles as I release, and my cum flows over my fingers. My eyes open, and the image of Lulu on her knees, covered in my cream, slowly dissolves.

I give a few final strokes until my balls are empty, but the want for Lulu doesn't subside. I can only imagine what could make this infernal want go away.

Maybe if I have her just once, this obsession with her will ease.

I shake my head to clear it. I know I wouldn't be so lucky. I understand that now. After just a single kiss, I recognized she would be like a slow poison dripping through my system. One I don't have an antidote for.

Prevention is better than the cure in this case.

I tidy myself up in my en suite bathroom, redressing in my suit. I'm at the sink mirror straightening my tie when I see movement in my bedroom from the open door.

My blood freezes in my veins, and I go still. My training comes into play quickly, and I finish straightening my tie without giving any sign of being caught off guard.

Angel stands in the doorway.

"What do you want?" I ask, fixing my cufflinks. I don't like that I didn't hear him enter.

"I don't know why you're here, but I want you to leave."

I turn to Angel and leisurely button my suit jacket. Jutting out my chin, I manage a thin smile. "Is that so?"

"Yeah, that's fucking so. I see how you look at my sister. My father won't stand for it."

I shoulder past Angel. Only moments ago, in the kitchen, I had wanted to throttle him, but that was before I got my emotions under control. Honestly, it would have been a mistake.

I fold my arms across my chest and keep my grin in place. I might not be willing to touch him—yet—but that doesn't mean I have to play nice.

"Why don't you run along, Angel. Let your father and I do the grown-up work."

It takes him two seconds to lose his temper. So predictable. He storms toward me, face red and veins bulging along his neck. "You think he would allow scum like you near Lulu?" His words are meant to send a dagger through my heart, but Angel has always been a very foolish boy.

"Lulu is worth much more," I say, agreeing with him. Then I jab. "Unlike you."

He swings. I dance back and avoid the punch. Dropping my arms, I go on the defensive.

He launches himself at me in a senseless rage. Never fight in anger; it's rule number one. Lose your temper, lose your head. That was my instructor's motto, and my instructor was the best there was even if he had been an asshole—my *padre*. I move to the side at the last second, sending Angel sailing into the wall by the force of momentum. His hands take the brunt of the fall, but the corner of his head makes contact.

"You should leave before you embarrass yourself further," I say.

He pulls himself upright and runs toward me, but I don't move completely out of his way this time. He would be expecting that. Instead, I spin to the opposite side, and before he knows what's happening, my arm collides with his chest, taking the wind right out of his lungs. He tumbles to the ground, breathless, and I sink a knee onto his chest. Gripping his tie, I yank it as he fights for air.

"If you ever come near me again, I will make you disappear." I release him and stand up. "*Capisce?*"

He gasps out something unintelligible, but I think I've gotten the message through Angel's thick skull. He nods and darts from my room like a wounded animal.

I run my hands through my hair and return to the window. I scan the yard for Vivi, but she isn't there anymore. As much as it hurts, I know I've made the right decision to walk away from Vivi and Lulu for now. They are a weakness I can't afford.

CHAPTER SIX

LULU

SO, THAT'S WHAT IT feels like to be kissed—truly kissed.

I'd been the recipient of a kiss or two before, but they were fumbling, distant memories in comparison to what just took place with Damon.

Damon's kiss... it devoured me as much as it adored me, and I want more.

I run from the kitchen, leaving the bread sitting about in its various stages. Someone else will come upon the mess and clean it for me, and I can't bring myself to be sorry for leaving things like that. I need my room, need to close my door and fall into my bed and hug a pillow to me while I take a minute—just a minute—to relive the utter magic of that kiss.

I almost make it.

Father stops me just as I reach the foyer, with its curving staircase that leads upstairs to the bedrooms. "Luciana!" His voice booms across the marble-tiled expanse, halting me with one foot on the first step. I sigh and turn to face him.

Hopefully, my face doesn't show what I've just been up to. "Good morning, Father."

"I'm looking for Damon. He didn't answer his phone when I called. Have you seen him?"

My cheeks heat, but I force my expression to remain neutral. "I did see him earlier. He was on the terrace with Vivi."

He was also in the kitchen. With his mouth on mine, making me feel all sorts of delicious—

Father nods to himself, rocking back on his heels. "Ah. He's good with your sister, I've noticed."

"Yes."

He's good with me, also.

With Angel... not so much. The thought reminds me of the almost wolfish expression I caught when Damon faced off with Angel. He was itching for Angel to make a move, to give him the excuse he needed to thrash him.

"Father..." I stop him as he moves to walk away.

He turns and raises an inquiring brow at me. "Yes?"

"I..." I swallow, tentative about how to proceed. I don't want to say anything that could land Damon in trouble, but my instincts are screaming that there's something we don't know. I don't know if it's a personal situation between him and Angel or something bigger, but the thought of it is like an itch beneath my skin.

"Well? I haven't got all day," Father says, impatient as always. In the end, I fumble, going with something else altogether.

"I just wondered if there was anything I could help you with." The words topple over themselves in their rush to be spoken.

Father simply looks at me, seeming confused. Then he waves a hand and turns, striding across the foyer toward the arched hallway that leads to his office. "Just find me Damon."

I watch him go and tell myself it's irritation I feel at being treated as though I'm twelve.

Not hurt.

***

"Why on earth you wanted to come here to shop, I'll never understand." I mutter a prayer for patience when a tourist bumps into me for the umpteenth time, too busy gawking at the Midtown majesty of Bloomie's to pay attention to other people.

"They have everything, that's why." Vivi shrugs. "And you said it yourself—I need it all."

"Yeah, I guess I did. Stop for a second, though. Let me fix this shoe."

Agreeably, Vivi steps a few feet away to study the window display while I sit on a nearby bench.

My sock has been pestering me all morning, refusing to stay in place and continually sliding down into the space created by the arch of my foot against the short boot I'm wearing. I fix it now, glancing up as I do to keep Vivi in my sights.

She's chattering away about some purse in the window, and I watch her with a half-smile, enjoying her bright company. It's so good to see her like this, free of worry and drama, and childlike in her enthusiasm.

She's been a bit down lately, as apparently Damon has been avoiding her as religiously as he has me.

I glance away, looking down the avenue at the flood of humanity coursing along, focused on this or that thing that occupies their attention. New York is always like this, loud and chaotic and *busy*. I would much rather be on our large but quiet estate on Staten Island, but the busyness is serving its purpose, I suppose. This is the first time I've thought of Damon in the past hour.

Something catches my eye as I people watch—something out of place.

There it is.

Roughly twenty to thirty yards away, in the shadowy alcove of a building, Angel is engaged in some sort of passionate discussion with several other men.

I frown. My brother does not look happy. He seems outright agitated, his hands speaking their own language in rapid-fire gestures while his lips move without ceasing. While he's talking to only one of the men, there are several more around him, all of them dressed in the kind of clothing that blends in with a crowd—jeans, hoodies, boots. Practiced at scanning for such things, I can easily make out the subtle lines of concealed weapons.

I don't recognize any of them as known enemies to the Valachi *famiglia*, but this is no gathering of friends.

"Have you noticed anything weird with Damon lately?" Vivi asks, coming to sit beside me on the bench. Oblivious to Angel's nearby presence, she plops a shopping bag between us and digs into its contents. I drag my attention back to her, trying to continue surreptitiously watching my brother at the same time. What had she...?

Oh, yes. Damon. Dannare.

"Ah... maybe? I'm not sure. What do you mean?"

She pulls out a new lip gloss and unscrews the cap, then uses her phone camera to apply it. "I feel like he's been avoiding me. It's weird. He never wants to do anything anymore."

I close my eyes on a slow blink before opening them and glancing over at Angel. "He's there to do a job, Vivi. Not be our friend."

"I know that," she grumbles. "It's just...he was our friend, you know? Or at least, he acted like he was."

And that's probably one hundred percent my fault. I turn my head so she won't see my expression.

"I wouldn't take it personally, Vivi. Father was looking for him the other day after you guys were on the terrace. Maybe he said something to him. You know how he is."

Vivi makes a tiny sound of agreement. "Hey, is that Angel? What—"

It looks as though the tension level in the little group down the street has risen several degrees. The jut of Angel's chin is distinctly combative. "It is. Stay here."

Without further analysis, I stand and approach the circle of men. I don't know what's going on, but I don't like the looks of the group. A closer study confirms my earlier opinion—I don't recognize any of them, which is alarming. As the son of the head of the Valachi crime syndicate, Angel has to use some caution for whom he's seen with. The network of our allies and enemies is vast and bewildering, especially as an individual's status can move from one to another in the space of minutes.

Being seen with the wrong person could put a target on all our backs.

"Angel!" I call, trying to divert attention and defuse the situation. Heads lift and eyes track my progress as I grow near, and I realize belatedly, as Angel's gaze widens on something behind me, that Vivi must have followed.

"*Fangoolo*," Angel says, breaking the tense silence hovering over the group at my arrival. All of the men immediately form a protective group around the one who seems to be in charge, ranks becoming obvious when they do. That one there—he's second-in-command of this motley crew. Those two—they're lesser soldiers.

It tells me what I need to know, though. This is no social club.

The men eye me boldly, one of them stepping forward and wiping at his bottom lip with a dirty thumb. "Well, well," he says. "What have we here?"

I only barely resist the urge to roll my eyes.

So original.

"What the *cazzo* are you doing here?" Angel tosses the cigarette he was using more as a crutch than actually smoking to the ground and stubs it out. Shoving past one of the men just in front of him, he grabs my shoulders and pushes me a couple steps away.

"We were shopping, *fratello*," I answer coolly. "What about you? Strange place for a meeting."

I don't like the way one of the men in particular is watching Vivi. She edges slightly further behind me, crowding against my back as two of them break ranks and circle to stand behind us.

"*Hola*, pretty." One with heavy tattooing reaches out a finger and trails it along Vivi's cheek.

She flinches, and I slap his hand away.

"Don't touch her," Angel says. He shoves the man, and instantly, another grips his shoulders, pulling him back.

"Feisty." The man I think of as the leader doesn't break eye contact with me. He has been menacing but quiet to this point, watching the action unfold with a reptilian gaze. Now he tilts his head to the side, tapping a finger against his chin as he considers something. Several inked tears drip beneath both eyes, and the image of a cross disappears into the collar of the shirt he wears. "I like her, Angelus."

I don't like the way he says Angel's full name—technically correct, but with a sibilant Latin accent.

"Yeah? Like it from a distance. We're leaving." I put an arm out, a silent command to Vivi to stay behind me and a warning to anyone interested in crossing it. I tip my chin, outwardly calm as I start to move both of us to the side, away from the men who surround us. Inwardly, though, I'm a mess.

This was a mistake.

I should have ignored Angel when I saw him.

What I shouldn't have done was come over and interrupt something that was obviously none of my business. But what the hell is Angel into? These men scream cartel. I don't know which one, but in general, the cartels around here are organizations that, as far as I know, the Valachi family doesn't mess with. They're all drugs and nastiness Father has always told me he wants no part of, including brutal slayings of their enemies and twisted dealings with their associates.

Did he lie to me? Are we in bed with the cartels, and I don't even know it?

"Not so fast." The leader's statement has the men closing around Vivi and me once again, forcing us further back into the alley we stand at the entrance of. I narrow my eyes as he shifts his attention to Angel. "You owe me a debt," he says, voice low.

Angel swallows. "I'll get you what you want—"

The other man's reply stops him. "Not good enough," he says. "The time for that is past. Leave the girls with us—"

"The hell I will—" Angel says.

"No!" I gasp a response. Behind me, Vivi goes statue still, a tiny whine escaping her lips.

Hands descend on my shoulders, pulling me farther into the alley. An SUV idles several yards away; windows blacked out. "Angel—"

He swivels his head to look at me, his eyes wild, noticeably shaken. "Carlos, enough! This is not what we agreed upon—"

"Whether you saw it coming or not makes no difference, *pendejo*."

I struggle against the hands that grip me, managing to twist around to face my assailant. Another man tugs at an unresistant Vivi, and I reach out to grab her and pull her close. She's murmuring to herself and entirely zoned out, as she's done a time or two in the past when we've been in a dangerous situation. Turtling, I call it. She curls into herself and hides until the danger is over.

It comes from a lifetime of exposure to violence, and the instinctive understanding that sometimes the only safety is in hiding.

Now is not the time to turtle, Vivi.

The one holding me claws at my arms, trying to get a better grip as I struggle against him, and behind us, I hear a scuffle break out, laced with low exclamations and grunts.

Bloomingdale's. This is happening right outside Bloomingdale's.

A gunshot rings out, checking my inane thoughts. It's loud and unmistakable in the alley, even suppressed by a silencer, and several others follow in the space of seconds. I whip my head around to see Angel, gun in hand, clutching his thigh where a wound pumps blood swiftly. Angel sinks to one knee alongside the tear-tatted orchestrator of this chaos, whose open eyes stare sightlessly at the sky.

He's been shot. They've both been shot. The cartel man is dead, and—

My brother's been shot. "Angel!" The scream rips out of me, loud, shrill.

A hand covers my mouth, and I bite down viciously. He jerks away with an oath, and I'm free suddenly. I can run, get away... but—

"Vivi! Come on!" I grab at my sister, but the man holding her simply pulls her inexorably closer to the waiting vehicle.

I sob in frustration.

Distantly, I hear the sound of a car squealing to the curb. Men scatter, and the one dragging Vivi suddenly pushes her into my arms and runs. I turn my head and see Damon—*Damon!*—leaping into the chaos like an avenging angel. He dispatches a quick, merciless bullet into each the heads of the remaining men and then hustles Vivi into the SUV waiting at the curb, engine running. He bends and scoops Angel up by the armpits and drags him efficiently to the same destination, where he pushes him up and into the back seat as Vivi scrambles out of the way.

Then he's standing before me, his warmth reaching out to comfort me, his fingers curving around the back of my neck and pulling me to his chest in a quick, hard embrace before he's pushing me, too, into the car.

He runs around the hood and slides into the driver's seat, pulling swiftly into traffic with a restrained growl of the engine. He places a hand on my thigh and squeezes briefly before returning it to the wheel, looking at me a single time as he makes his way out of the city. The depths of his gaze are plagued with something like desperation.

I close my eyes and lay my head back against the headrest.

I recognize it, that desperation. I feel it, fueled by the same hunger and fear and helplessness that races through my body.

Relentless.

Eternal.

CHAPTER SEVEN

DAMON

N O ONE SPEAKS FOR a full five minutes as we speed back to the Valachi mansion. Shock still ricochets through each of us, keeping us quiet. Lulu is the one to break the silence, shouting at me.

"Stop the car!"

I slam on the brakes. What the hell is wrong? Was she shot? Did I miss something?

Dear God, no. I mumble to myself as I pull to the curb. Please be okay…

She unbuckles her belt. "I need to be with Vivi," she explains as she jumps out and gets into the back. Vivi hasn't stopped crying, and Angel is doing nothing to comfort his sister. His focus is on his leg. He had better not bleed out before I can kill him.

Once Lulu is resettled in the back of the SUV, squatting in the floorboard because there's no space to sit, I pull back out onto the road. I watch as she takes Vivi's cheeks in her palms, whispering something fiercely to her. Whatever she says, it makes Vivi settle back into the seat and work on curbing her tears.

Lulu turns to Angel next, who's stretched as much as he can be across the back seat.

"Where is it, Angel?" she asks. He gestures with a limp hand to his thigh, and she begins probing with delicate fingers at the site.

"How bad is it, *bella*?" I ask.

Her worried gaze meets mine in the rearview mirror. "I think it's just a heavy graze, but it's hard to tell."

"Hurts like fucking hell," Angel says. His voice wobbles, and I wonder if it's the first time he's been shot.

Lulu uses Angel's belt to tourniquet the wound and then squeezes in beside her sister on the seat, pushing her closer to their brother. He hisses as they jar his leg, but he doesn't say anything else. I divide my gaze between the road in before me and Lulu in the rearview mirror. Her skin is flushed, and she fidgets with her hands. Her gaze darts out the various windows like she's looking for a threat.

"You're safe," I inform her.

Her gaze snaps to mine. The pulse of fear flickers in her neck. I keep eye contact as long as I can before I have to revert my attention to the road. I tighten my hands on the steering wheel, my knuckles turning white.

Vivi starts to cry again and is shushed by Lulu. I risk another peek to see Lulu embrace her sister, giving her comfort by stroking her hair. I can't bring myself to look at Angel again. He's some bastard for putting them in danger like that. I already hated him, but this brought his worth to a new low in my books.

"We're nearly there," I say out loud. I'm not sure what I'm trying to calm, my raging need for bloodshed or Vivi's constant, soft weeping.

The wrought iron gates to the mansion come into view, and I slow the vehicle down. The gates seem slower today, and I'm tempted to rev the engine in warning for them to move faster. Instead, I exercise the control my father instilled in me.

The gates finally grant me enough access to the driveway, and I press down on the accelerator, yanking pebbles from their slumber as I tear up the drive. The moment I'm at the door, I'm out of the vehicle. I should get the girls inside, but my control is slipping as I round the car to Angel's door.

He's cowering in the backseat. The air rushes in and stirs Lulu's long locks, sending some strands across her flushed cheeks. Through her hair, I see the terror still lurking like a bad dream in her eyes.

Unacceptable.

Reaching in, I grip Angel by the scruff of the neck and drag him from the car. His feet don't quite land, and I'm dragging him toward the mansion. He manages to right his footing and is hobbling with his injured leg by the time Lulu busts from the car.

"Damon, what are you doing?" Her panic has her running until she's in front of me. She pushes long tendrils out of her face and straightens to her full height. "Let him go! He's been shot!"

"Not now, *bella*." I don't have the patience for this. Angel will answer to his father for putting Vivi and Lulu in danger, and if Lorenzo doesn't take care of matters, I will. This won't happen again.

"Let me go." Angel's protest is weak, like a man who knows he's rightly fucked.

I tighten my hold on his neck and shake him, hoping he can feel the anger I'm withholding for Lulu's sake. No one else's.

"Move, *bella*," I say, as Lulu stays rooted to the spot in front of me. I could walk around her, but I'm giving her a chance. "I won't harm him. But he has to answer to your father."

I want to beat him within an inch of his life, but I will refrain from exercising my true wants.

"Lulu!" Vivi bursts from the car, released from her state of shock. She rushes past me and slams her shaking frame into Lulu's arms.

"He will answer for what he did one way or another," I inform Lulu. She wraps her arms around her sister, and her gaze darts to the left, freeing me from standing here with a wriggling Angel.

I move past Lulu and into the house. Angel doesn't fight me, and I don't release him until I open his father's study door and drop him to his knees. He gasps then, a hand flying to his thigh to suppress the new flux of blood.

"What in God's name?" Lorenzo Valachi rises from behind his desk, removing a pair of black-framed reading glasses from his face. "What is the meaning of this?"

He's looking from me to Angel, but as he sees the blood on Angel's trousers, his expression hardens, devoid of any warmth or sympathy for his son. He knows. Angel is his son, but he knows what he is. Useless. A fool.

"Why don't you tell your father what you have been up to?" I want to kick Angel on the floor but find my control and remain still.

Angel starts mumbling. "I'm sorry, Papa... I messed up."

I step closer to him, and he cowers again. My gaze moves to his father, who's waiting.

"He nearly got Lulu and Vivi killed. He was making side deals with the local dealers. Deals he has no right to make."

Angel is rising, holding out both his hands while shaking his head. He hobbles forward and hisses before speaking. "I didn't bring the girls, *padre*. They weren't supposed to be there." The plea in Angel's voice makes me feel sorry for him for a split second, until I remember seeing Lulu in the line of fire.

"You did what?" Lorenzo takes a step toward him.

"I wanted to make a deal with them myself. Show you what I can do." Angel fixes his crumbled shirt from being manhandled. "They shouldn't have been there." He points at me as if it's my fault. "They should have been here at home, safe."

I don't look away as Lorenzo's hand lands heavily on Angel's face. The crack of flesh hitting flesh makes me flinch internally.

Angel holds his face. "I was trying to make you proud." He sounds like the broken little boy he is.

"Local drug dealers. You think that would make me proud? My son, a drug dealer?" Lorenzo's chuckle holds not one ounce of humor.

Angel's face is beet red, and when he glances at me, I see his hate.

"You are an embarrassment to this family," Lorenzo declares.

Angel fumbles with more words but ceases as his father strikes him again. "Such a disappointment. God cursed me with you!"

I internally wince again, the sound reminding me too much of my own relationship with my father, but I refuse to have pity for a creature like Angel. Angel is ready to flee, but his father thumps his fist on the mahogany writing desk. "You will tell me the deal you made with them so I can clean up your mess."

"It was one shipment that they would distribute for me."

"I have men for that." Lorenzo shakes his head before pinching the bridge of his nose. I'm wondering when he will ask if his daughters are safe, but that seems to be the furthest from his mind.

"The profits would have been better if I had done it directly." Angel defends his stupid decision, and another strike to his face has him holding his swollen red cheek.

"Imbecile. We have men in place to keep our hands clean." Lorenzo looks at me for the first time. "You will have to fix this."

I nod. "I have disposed of all the men who were present, but I will make it right with the local cartel and law enforcement."

Angel opens his mouth to protest but wisely closes it.

"Get out of my sight and clean yourself up," Lorenzo demands.

Angel leaves, slinking from the room like a wounded animal, but not before giving me a look loaded with pure hate. I return the sentiment.

Lorenzo sinks into his chair, sighing heavily. "That's it. I'm done with the boy. He will no longer have a say in the family business. And I have a meeting with all the Valachi coming up." He strokes two fingers across his left brow. "You will attend with me."

Surprise flitters through my system. This is it. This is my opportunity to get to meet all the men of the Valachi. If it wasn't Lorenzo, one of them ordered my mother's death. I would finally come face-to-face with the man who tore everything away from me.

I nod. "Whatever you need."

Excitement pours through my veins. This is what I have been waiting for. This moment in time. An opportunity couldn't have presented itself so neatly, so I guess I should be thankful to Angel for being such a fuckup. This is only the first step, but it will grant me an audience with these men, and slowly, with time and the right strategy, I will find out who took my mother's light from me. I will destroy this family from the inside out. I will leave them throneless and empty-handed.

Brick by brick, I will tear them apart.

"Thank you, Damon. We Italians need to stick together, watch out for one another. I consider you *famiglia* now, you know." Lorenzo's gaze doesn't waver as he stares at me.

Outwardly, I smile. Inwardly, I sneer in disgust. He has no idea of the meaning of family. What we Papparado had was *famiglia*. I push those thoughts away and nod again at him. "And I consider you *famiglia*, as well."

Liar.

He walks to me and places his hands on my shoulders, dragging my frame down so he can press kisses to either cheek. It's a traditional greeting for family. My mind skips to the last memory of my mother placing this same kind of soft kiss on my cheeks. When Lorenzo releases me, I know I've had all of his presence that I can stomach.

"*Grazie*," Lorenzo says as he returns to his desk.

I leave the room, breathing harshly through my nose once the door closes behind me. I need to tell Marcus about the change, of course, for us. He keeps watch on everything, so I can't keep how things have transpired from him. It's almost here... our time to crush them. And we will, slowly and painfully. Our revenge won't be swift or merciful. No, it will be dragged out, and they won't even know what's happening until it's too late.

***

It's taken me two days to negotiate with the local cartel. The police were easier. But with enough money and the promise of repercussions for Angel, their leader finally accepts my offer of recompense for the deaths of his men and the spoiled shipment. Lorenzo hadn't stated what power I had to clear up this mess, but I'm sure everything was at my disposal, and I didn't want to spend too much time with the scum of the streets.

"Is that you, Damon?" A voice laced with alcohol and mockery comes from the main drawing room.

I could keep walking and pretend I don't hear Lulu's drunk mother, but I'm bored. I use my foot to push open the door. Leaning against the doorframe, I stare at this sorry excuse of a mother.

She blinks and stands. The martini glass in her hand is empty, which is good because if it weren't, it would be sloshed across the floor.

"Have you seen my boy?" She blinks several times, a false eyelash crooked on her cheek.

"Your cat?" I ask, fucking with her.

Her eyes widen. "My cat?" She's far more intoxicated than I thought.

"Yes, the black-and-white tomcat. Is that who you're looking for? If so, I haven't seen him." There is no cat, but that's of no consequence.

She shakes her head and steps forward. The martini glass is upside down by the time she reaches me. Her leopard print shirt is too tight, her artificial breasts pouring from atop the straining buttons.

"My boy, *Angel*. He hasn't been seen for two days."

I push off the doorframe.

That's an interesting development.

I shake my head. "I haven't seen him."

She waves the glass in the air. "I'm sure he will turn up. *I ragazzi saranno ragazzi.*"

Boys will be boys. I want to smirk at that. Angel is no boy. He's a menace. "Yeah. I'm sure he will show up soon."

She shrugs. "Don't strain yourself to help."

I turn away from her as she sits back down. "I won't," I mumble.

I leave the drawing room, only to find Lulu standing like a regal queen in the hallway. Her head is held high, and the extravagant plaits that wrap around her head make her look ethereal.

I want to walk past her. I haven't spoken to her since the incident the other day. I'm trying to create distance. Going after her family won't be easy if she's always looking at me with her pretty hazel eyes, just like she's looking at me now.

"What's on your mind?" I ask instead. I can't help myself when it comes to Lulu, not after that kiss. It was... unexpected. Even more unexpected was how it ramped up my lust for her to impossible degrees.

I can wait, though. Knowing she will be mine one day keeps my want at bay.

"My brother is on my mind."

So direct. I smother a smirk.

"Yes. On your mother's, as well. She informed me he has been missing for two days. I'm sure he will turn up." I walk past her, but her small hand touches my forearm, freezing me.

"I know you have your differences, but something is wrong. I can feel it."

I glance down at her. "Feel it?" I question.

Her cheeks heat up, but she doesn't shy away. "Angel has never been gone for longer than a few hours. He won't answer his phone. I've checked his room, and nothing is missing. Which means he didn't run away. Something has happened."

And since when is this my problem? I'm delighted he's gone. I work on keeping my face neutral. It isn't Lulu's fault her brother is a deadbeat asshole.

"You should take your concerns to your father." I glance down at her hand still resting on my forearm, and Lulu removes it, finger by finger, before dropping her hands to her side.

"I have spoken to my father, but he has no care for Angel. That's why I'm asking you, Damon."

I glance around the hallway before I turn back to Lulu. "Asking me what?"

"I want you to find him for me." She's staring right into my eyes.

She is truly my weakness. I can't deny her. Finding Angel wouldn't be a major problem for me; his father has already disowned him, and he won't be coming back, not if the don doesn't allow it. Even if he did return, he would never exercise the kind of authority I already possess. If nothing else, Angel can always be a distraction and a reminder to Lorenzo of my value.

"For you, *bella*, I will find Angel."

Her eyes snap open, and gratitude fills them.

"But make no mistake—this is the last favor I will grant you." I think I need to say it more for myself than her.

Lulu takes a tiny step away from me. The action is minuscule, but I notice everything about her.

"*Grazie*, Damon."

I nod and walk away from her. I would do her this one final grace as a gift.

As for myself... I'll dream of her while I wreak my revenge on her family. Maybe after I win this war, I will be able to claim my prize.

Lulu.

CHAPTER EIGHT

LULU (FIVE YEARS LATER - Present Day)

T HE WATER LAPS GENTLY at my shoulders and the tops of my breasts as I sit back in the Jacuzzi on our terrace. I'm naked beneath the surface of the water, but it's dark, and no one's ever around to see me, so it's a habit I've developed. If Vivi happens to be peering out her window, or if someone strolls out onto the terrace, I can always just stay in the water to avoid giving them an eyeful.

It's been an exhausting day, one I'm ready to rinse off and be done with. I close my eyes and allow the sounds of the evening to settle softly all around me.

Night birds sing one another to sleep, and the water gurgles its own quiet song. The faint strains of music pulsing from Vivi's open window upstairs provide accompaniment, and behind the wall of shrubbery, the heating and cooling system hums quietly.

White noise, all of it, and so soothing, especially paired with the faint chill of the spring evening. I could fall asleep if I allowed myself to do so, but I'm still too tense.

I met with the wife of one of Father's soldiers today. The girl was young, in her early twenties, and the meeting was unsettling. It was like looking into a mirror and seeing myself as I had been several years ago—unsettled and unhappy and wanting more.

So much more.

The soldier's wife couldn't understand why her husband wasn't allowing her to go to college. All she wanted, after all, was to earn a degree and have some opportunity to make a name for herself. It was clear to me that she had no concept of the life she had married into, what it entailed, what it demanded from its men and its women and its children—all of us.

I soothed her as best I could and sent her on her way. And then, I left a note for Damon to speak with her husband. He needed to find a method of encouraging her and making her feel significant in her own right, if la famiglia was going to keep her from pursuing her dream. It wasn't a perfect solution, but it would help a bit.

My nerve endings perk to life suddenly and send a tickle along my skin, where my hair stands at attention. There's something different in the atmosphere. Without opening my eyes, I know it is Damon. His presence calls to mine, and I've come to understand that I'd recognize him in a crowded room if I were blind and deaf.

Opening my eyes, I turn my head against the back of the spa and see him, a black silhouette hovering on the fringes of the terrace, one among the shadows. He separates himself from the backdrop of darkness and steps forward, slowly easing himself down to sit on the chaise lounge beside the tub. Without speaking, he leans forward and rests his forearms on his thighs, allowing his hands to dangle loosely between his legs.

Tension arcs between us, fairly sparking as he catches and holds my gaze with his. I shiver a bit and look away, deliberately allowing my chest to bob a bit out of the water. His eyelids droop as his gaze drops reflexively, the tip of his tongue darting out to lick his lips.

I smile to myself. Damon has worked religiously to ignore me for these past five years, but the temptation has always been there, mocking him and frustrating me.

If I could have just one person—other than Vivi, of course—want me and choose me regardless of my family's name, it would be Damon. Such wishes are for fools, though.

"I see you finally decided to join the household once again," I say, unable to keep the edge out of my voice. Damon has been gone for four days, giving us no word of explanation or even telling us when he planned to return. I had no idea where he was, no idea how to get in contact with him, as he didn't seem to be receiving any of my messages. "Father's been sick and asking for you, you know."

He drops his head and looks at his hands, turning each palm to the sky like they contain the secrets of the universe. "I am aware," he says.

That's it. Just...

I am aware.

Irritation rolls through me, making me narrow my eyes and sit up a bit straighter in the bubbling water. His glance moves again to the hint of wet flesh and then lifts back to mine, unperturbed.

They're hot, though, those eyes. Banked embers burn, turning the air around us to steam.

"These little side trips of yours, the ones you take without telling me, without giving me any explanation... they need to stop." I don't know where the words come from. They're sparked, I suppose, by my aggravation that I've been left to deal with everything on my own and his refusal to explain or apologize for it. This is his *job*.

"Spoken like a true queen," he murmurs, almost to himself.

"What's that supposed to mean?"

"It's of no consequence," he says, then continues on a sigh. "And I had matters to attend to."

I relax back, the fight gone. He seems weary. Unhappy, even. "It's fine, Damon. Father... he just wanted you, and you weren't here. There's something wrong with him."

He's been ailing for weeks, but whatever is making him ill has taken a sharp downturn this week. He's spent the time in bed, his room dark and smelling of sour flesh and sickness, even though the staff has tended to his every physical need.

"I think he needs a different doctor," I say, voicing the thought uppermost in my mind. "Whatever this one is doing doesn't seem to be working."

Damon's eyes close briefly, then open. He stands and turns, slipping his hands into his pockets, then slowly, he turns back to face me. "Lulu... your father is dead."

He ignores my sharp gasp, the water splashing as my hands fly up to cover my mouth, to prevent any of the craziness in my head from escaping.

No. Yes. What now? What comes next?

Everything.

Everything comes now.

He keeps going, strangely passionless, grimly efficient in his task of telling me my father is dead. "He passed quietly and comfortably just this past hour. I'm very sorry, Lulu."

"Sorry."

He's sorry. I can't prevent the huff of laughter that explodes from my lips. If he only knew the terrible thoughts running through my mind right now, he wouldn't be telling me how sorry he is.

Father is dead, and instead of feeling grief, I feel *free*. Lorenzo Valachi is gone, and I can do whatever I want—I can *be* whomever I want to be.

I clear my throat. "How did he die?"

"I'm not certain, but from some things he hinted at, I think it was a brain tumor. I ordered an autopsy, so we'll know more shortly."

I let out a low hum of response.

A brain tumor. It makes sense. There were days, this past year in particular, that I thought he had completely lost his mind. He was gambling, and though he kept it relatively quiet, he was losing. And I'm pretty sure Damon was scrambling to douse fires Father had started with some of the crazy things he'd said.

"I don't know what to do now," I say into the silence that has fallen between us. "What does this mean? For me? For Vivi? Our mother..." I laugh again, an ugly sound without mirth. Mother doesn't leave her room most days. She has all the company she needs in there—her good friends Gin, Vodka, and Tequila. "And God, Angel. He won't even know..."

Dannaro.

There are probably a dozen things I need to be doing right now. I stand, unconcerned with my nakedness as the water sluices down. Damon startles, his eyes going wide. He raises his chin as I face him for a second without speaking.

"*Madre de Dio,*" he mutters, voice thick. "*Bellissim—*"

Placing a hand on the side, I start to climb out. Water blinds me, and I misstep, one foot slipping on the stone floor as I start to go down, and the other hooking around the side of the tub.

I don't fall, though. Damon catches me, pulling me easily over the edge and into his chest, his arms sliding around my back to hold me firmly in place. He's wearing casual clothing tonight, sweatpants and a tee shirt that's soft against my cheek. His fingers flex on my wet flesh, moving against it as if driven by instinct.

God, he's strong. And warm. Shivers start to rack my frame, and Damon shifts, picking up the towel I tossed over the chaise earlier before wrapping it around me. He tucks it with exaggerated care into a knot at my neck, then sets me away from him. A long, considering look into my face has him swiping his thumbs across my cheekbones, and I realize I'm crying.

"Why am I crying?" I wonder aloud. "He was not a good father—"

"But maybe he wasn't a complete bastard, either, now was he?" Damon soothes, pulling me back against him. If I didn't know better, I'd say he likes holding me.

But I don't want his comfort. I don't want his coddling, his care. I twist away and start pacing the short segment of the terrace that houses the hot tub, the towel flapping around me with each step.

"No!" I return. "He was a bastard. Did you know I wanted to go to culinary school and become a chef? But he wouldn't allow it because I was... this... thing. This possession for him to do with as he pleased. Angel was never good enough, and Vivi was too young, and so I gave up everything to be what he needed me to be." I fling a hand toward Damon. "Which apparently was not what I thought he needed, because along came you."

"Lulu—"

I pick up the wineglass I set on the rim of the tub earlier, then take a long swig of the remaining wine. "Everything, Damon. I gave it all up without complaint. I dealt with Mother, handled Angel, practically raised my sister—all for what? Now the reason for that is gone. And you know as well as I do, that it's all going to continue to fall on my shoulders. In spite of everything, aside from you being here, there is no one else."

I stop talking and study the empty wineglass in my hand, the way it catches tiny points of light from various sources, and then I hurl it at the stone wall of the terrace. It shatters into a thousand tiny shards of glass, and I crumple. I sink to my knees, the towel tangled around me, and a rough, shredded wail breaks free of my throat.

"*Dio, bella*. Please don't cry. I can't—" Damon lowers himself to the ground and pulls me into his lap. One hand curves around my wet hair, pinning my face to his chest, and I cry wordlessly into the softness of his tee shirt for what feels like an eternity.

Finally, my tears come to a halt with a watery sniffle, and I lean back a little to wipe at my face and then the wet spot on his shirt. "*Dio*, I'm sorry. Ugh. I just... I just want to be free of it all, Damon."

He tilts my face back, his long fingers warm and strong on my jaw. His gaze traces everything—my still leaking eyes, the tremble of my mouth, the hands that clutch at his shirt to prevent him from letting me go. After a moment that lasts a lifetime, he replies.

"That's not the world we live in, *bella*."

My breath catches at the tenderness in his voice, at odds with what he's saying, and a knot twists and tightens in my stomach as he continues.

"You'll never be free."

Do you want to continue Damon's and Lulu's journey?

Sign up to our newsletter to be notified when it releases HERE

Index for Italian words

Figlio - Son

Madre - Mother

Nonna - Grandmother

Zia - Aunt

Sorella - Sister

Padre - Father

Grazie - Thank you

Dio santo - Holy God

bella ragazza - Beautiful Girl/pretty girl

Dannare - Damn

Fratello - Brother

fotti - fuck

Famiglia - family

I ragazzi saranno ragazzi - Boys will be boys.

Stronzo - Asshole

Saluti – Greetings

Capische – do you understand

Gelato – ice cream

Fangoolo – fuck

About Vi Carter & E.R. Whyte

W HEN VI CARTER ISN'T writing contemporary & dark romance books, that feature the mafia, are filled with suspense, and take you on a fast paced ride, you can find her reading her favorite authors, baking, taking photos or watching Netflix.

Married with three children, Vi divides her time between motherhood and all the other hats she wears as an Author.

She has declared herself a coffee & chocolate addict! Do not judge.

E.R. Whyte is a multi-genre author, writing contemporary and new adult romance under E.R. Whyte, reverse harem romance under Evie Rae, and sweet romance under Elle Rae Whyte. Although it would no doubt make life easier to simply choose a genre, she loves romance in all its forms too much to ever do that.

She's a simple girl at heart, living in a teeny-tiny Virginia town and spending her time finding herself, catering to various fur babies, and indulging her reading, writing, and photography habits. She loves being alone, bananas foster, and Pepsi.

Whyte worked as a high school English teacher for around a decade before she decided she really wanted more time to devote to her family and other fun stuff. Now she thinks up new ways to make tacos on Tuesday, explores the Marvel universe with childish enthusiasm, and spends entirely too much time on the computer.

Life is good.

Social Media Links for Elle & Vi

Website

Facebook Reading Group

Tiktok

www.ingramcontent.com/pod-product-compliance
Lightning Source LLC
Chambersburg PA
CBHW030810190726
48285CB00003B/1112